HIGH TREASON AT
CATFISH BEND

Books by Ben Lucien Burman

HIGH TREASON AT CATFISH BEND

BLOW A WILD BUGLE FOR CATFISH BEND

THE OWL HOOTS TWICE AT CATFISH BEND

SEVEN STARS FOR CATFISH BEND

HIGH WATER AT CATFISH BEND

THE SIGN OF THE PRAYING TIGER

THE STREET OF THE LAUGHING CAMEL

THE FOUR LIVES OF MUNDY TOLLIVER

EVERYWHERE I ROAM

ROOSTER CROWS FOR A DAY

BLOW FOR A LANDING

STEAMBOAT ROUND THE BEND

MISSISSIPPI

THE GENERALS WEAR CORK HATS

IT'S A BIG CONTINENT

IT'S A BIG COUNTRY

CHILDREN OF NOAH

MIRACLE ON THE CONGO

BIG RIVER TO CROSS

High Treason
At Catfish Bend

Ben Lucien Burman

Illustrated by Alice Caddy

New York
Vanguard Press, Inc.

HIGH TREASON AT
CATFISH BEND

I was sitting in the shade of a spreading cottonwood at Catfish Bend, watching a towboat going down the Mississippi, when I saw two foxes come hurrying out of the nearby swamp, with four beavers a few paces behind. All of the six were strangers to the Bend, I could tell. And they were up to no good, I was certain. They kept turn-ing around every other step to make sure nobody was following. The older of the two foxes was some kind of gangster, you knew right off. He walked with a swagger as if he owned the place; his red fur was so care-fully combed and so shiny it looked as if he'd coated it with wax.

At an order from him each of the beavers went up to a tree and stood waiting.

"Chop!" called the fox, and the beavers with their long sharp teeth began to make big gashes in the tree trunks.

They'd been working a minute or two when I saw my old friend, Doc Raccoon, come running. His usually good-natured face with the black stripes around his eyes that made him look like a masked bank rob-ber was quivering with fury; he was breath-ing so hard I was afraid he was going to have a heart attack.

"Stop!" he shouted.

The beavers stopped chopping and then looked at the fox, not knowing what to do.

The raccoon rushed up to the fox. "What's the meaning of this?" he demanded.

The fox smiled a smile like that of an alligator when he's just about to catch a goose, then turned away so he wouldn't look the raccoon in the eye. "We're getting ready for the election," he said.

"The election isn't till this afternoon," sputtered the raccoon, so furious he could hardly talk. "Anyway you haven't won it yet. Get out."

The foxes and the beavers moved off.

The raccoon saw me and sat down by my side. "It's enough to drive you crazy. . . . You haven't got one of those nice jawbreaker candies, have you? I need something to hold my nerves in."

I always carry a bag of candy when I go to the Bend. "I couldn't get the jawbreak-

ers," I said. "But I've got a couple of licorice whips and some candy bananas. Maybe those'll help you."

"I'll take the licorice whips. They're hard and I've heard the snake doctors here talking. They say licorice is good for the stomach."

The raccoon broke off a piece of the licorice handle and washed it in the river, the way raccoons do with everything they eat.

"Who are those queer-looking foxes anyway?" I asked. "I wouldn't like to meet either of 'em down a dark alley."

The raccoon chewed the licorice thoughtfully. You could see right off he thought a lot. "They're city slickers from up North—Chicago or Detroit or somewhere. They came to Catfish Bend with the beavers a month ago. They're wonderful talkers and you know how silly people can be with good talkers. Animals are the same way."

"I heard you say something about an election. What's the election?"

The raccoon reached for the bag I was holding. "I think I'll try one of the candy bananas. Licorice whips aren't what they used to be. . . . I'll tell you about the election. But first I better tell you what went on before. It's the biggest thing we've ever had to decide on the river. If these foxes and the beavers win it'll be the end of Catfish Bend."

The raccoon began:

1

Most terrible things happen when you don't expect 'em, like getting hit by an automobile just when you're on your way back to your hole with the pecan pie you've borrowed from the farmer's wife in the house at the Bend after she put it on the back porch to cool. This awful business I'm going to tell you about happened so slow and easy nobody knew what was going on until it was too late. The first sign came one afternoon when our gloomy old frog was rehearsing the frogs of the Indian Bayou Glee Club.

"We're giving a concert in Sugar Cane next Tuesday," he said—Sugar Cane's the town nearest the Bend. "There are some visiting frogs from Okefenokee Swamp in Georgia have one of the finest glee clubs in the country and I want you to do your best. We'll start out with *Sweet Adeline*."

He'd scarcely finished talking when a young frog jumped up had only been in the Club a month. "I don't want to sing *Adeline* any more," he said. "I want to sing some of the new pieces with plenty of noise in 'em. Some frogs from the Hudson River in New York passed through the Bend yesterday on their way to California and sang some of the new pieces and they were wonderful."

"I'm tired of *Adeline* and I'm tired of Catfish Bend," said another young frog. "I want to go to California, like the others."

The wrinkles in the old frog's face turned gray; he started shivering as if he'd fallen into the river in winter. Nobody had ever talked to him that way before, particularly a frog in the Glee Club.

"It's the end of the world," he croaked.

The rest of us were as shocked as the old frog. Judge Black, the wonderful black-snake from Claiborne County, Mississippi, who was trying to live down the snake's bad reputation by becoming a vegetarian, looked at the young frogs as if he couldn't believe what he was hearing. His eyes were filled with tears; since he'd become a vegetarian he cried easily.

"Bad fruit will never taste sweet," he said. Being a judge he knew a lot of mottoes, though often like this time you couldn't figure out exactly what he meant. "A foolish son is his father's sorrow."

And then we found out all the young frogs felt the same way. "The frogs from New York say California is Heaven," squeaked a third young frog whose voice was changing. "They said why do you stay in a one-horse place like Catfish Bend where you have tornadoes and floods and droughts all the time, and the people are so mean and keep such tight lids on their garbage cans you cut your paws and break your teeth trying to get one open. In California the people love animals, they said, and put the lids on the cans so loose a tadpole can get them open."

"Catfish Bend and everybody in it is dead and doesn't know it," said a fourth young frog. "The New York frogs said they'd go crazy living in a place like Catfish Bend where they pull in the sidewalks when it gets dark."

"The frogs are right," said a young raccoon that I'd trained myself and I thought had good sense. "Everybody's going to California. Some raccoons passing through a few days ago said there's a stretch of land between San Francisco and Los Angeles they call Paradise Valley that's the most beautiful place in the world. They say there are so many melons and peaches and plums left in the fields and the orchards they're paying Mexicans to come and carry them away."

"People are going, too," said a young squirrel. "Hundreds of 'em. I was on the porch of one of the houses at the edge of the Bend near town, getting ready to borrow some strawberries on a table, and two old ladies were sitting there talking. They had pictures of the land people were selling in Paradise Valley and it looked like Heaven. The old ladies said they were going to sell their house and go there right away."

Well, the young frogs and the other young animals kept talking this way, getting more and more excited, till the old frog finally had to call off the rehearsal; the young ones wouldn't sing *Adeline* any more. And the old frog had to send word to Sugar Cane and cancel the concert. I should have guessed then that terrible times

were coming. Never before, since I'd been living at the Bend had a thing like that ever happened. When an animal at the Bend gave his word he kept it, no matter what the cost.

A few weeks passed and more and more animals came through on the way to California. And the young animals at the Bend got more and more restless and anxious to go there too. And pretty soon it wasn't just the young animals. The old ones began to talk the same way.

"Life's too hard here at the Bend for us old animals," said a turtle who'd lived so many years his shell was covered with moss. "In winter your head turns into an icicle; it's frozen so stiff you can hardly pull it back into your shell. In summer it's so hot you feel like a fried chicken. In Paradise Valley it's always just right."

"At Catfish Bend it's so noisy now with all the towboats going past on the river and the cars on the highway you can't get a wink of sleep," said an old possum. "A possum needs more sleep than anybody. In Paradise Valley they say the possums sleep day and night."

About this time two snow-white crows came flying in early one morning. They were husband and wife, they said, from the Yukon up in Canada; they asked if they could have a job at the Bend. 'Course we knew white crows were something special; all white crows can tell the weather, and

some can tell the future.

"We were the best prophets in all Canada," the husband said. "We were the ones who told about the big storm on the Great Lakes that sank all those ships and we told about the volcano that made the new island off Iceland. We told about the big hunting club was going to the Yukon to hunt the Rocky Mountain sheep, and we gave the

sheep plenty of time to hide so the hunters didn't get one. The animals in the Yukon begged us not to leave. But my wife has bad asthma and needs a warm climate."

You can't get prophets like that every day of the week, and the old owl who'd been prophesying at the Bend had died a few months before. We had a squirrel for a while

23

who said he couldn't tell the future, but told us he was a wonder at the weather. We let him try but when he'd say rain the day would be beautiful. When he'd say it would be hot all the animals would go swimming; instead we'd have a terrible blizzard and everybody 'd get pneumonia.

"Oh carrots!" giggled our silly rabbit, who'd been chasing a butterfly around a tree and came over to join in the discussion. "Let 'em stay. I like to hear crows caw. It's like listening to the new kind of music."

"The rabbit's right," said J.C., our sporty red fox from Memphis, the biggest show-off in the Mississippi Valley. "A white crow's good luck like the white rabbit's foot I always carry." He pulled out a worn rabbit's foot and poked it in the rabbit's stomach, then roared with laughter at his own joke. The rabbit turned pale and didn't giggle any more.

"Let them stay," said Judge Black.

"Friends are like money. They are easier made than kept."

Nobody knew quite what he meant but it sounded good.

The crows had been at the Bend a month, I guess, and every day the crowd of animals going to California got bigger. And then the drought came and the animals talked more and more about going to California. It wasn't a bad drought. We'd often had worse at the Bend. But it was enough to make things happen.

I was sitting under my favorite live oak one afternoon watching some black and red ants having such a terrible fight they didn't notice a lizard who'd have gobbled 'em all up if I hadn't called out, when I saw a crowd of the Catfish Bend animals coming toward me, with the young raccoon I'd trained myself and the young frogs in the Glee Club that wouldn't sing *Adeline* marching at the head. Behind them were all the other young

25

animals and most of the old ones at the Bend.

"We've just had a meeting," said the young raccoon. "And we've decided. We young animals won't stay in Catfish Bend any longer. We're going to Paradise Valley."

"We're going with 'em," said the old turtle with the moss on his shell. "We turtles should live to be two hundred years old.

I'm a hundred and twenty now and with this river dampness my rheumatism's so bad if I stayed I'd be lucky if I reached a hundred twenty-five."

"Carrots and asparagus!" said the silly rabbit who'd been pulling the petals off a sunflower, trying to tell his fortune. "Why don't we all go? Everything here's drying up. There isn't a decent piece of lettuce in a hundred miles."

I didn't answer the rabbit. He was too silly and didn't really count. I did argue with the others, but it did no good. After a few minutes they marched off to have another meeting.

The two white crows had come up beside me and they were so shocked they turned black, just as shocked black crows turn white. They didn't say anything, but early next morning they both hurried to where I was eating my breakfast with Judge Black and J.C. and the rabbit and the old frog.

The crows were shivering so hard they each shook loose half a dozen feathers.

They turned upside down and stood on their heads, and I knew they were going to prophesy. They told me they learned this from some mynah birds who'd worked for some priests called Yogis in India. The Yogis said standing on your head made the prophesying much better.

"I had a dream last night," said the husband. "I saw the Catfish Bend animals on the way to Paradise Valley. They were singing as they marched along, happy as love-birds on the way to a wedding. And suddenly I saw a flock of buzzards come, so many the sky grew inky black, like it does in a terrible storm. And they rushed over my head with a roar like a tornado, and settled on the ground where the animals had been marching. And then I saw the reason why. The Catfish Bend animals were lying there, like they were made of stone. Every one was dead."

The wife spoke up now. "I had a dream the same time," she said. "I saw the Catfish Bend animals marching, happy the same way. And suddenly instead there were only howling coyotes, thick as ants. And the Catfish Bend animals weren't animals any more. They were only white skeletons shining in the moon."

The husband tried to stop shivering but couldn't. "We've had this double dream twice before. Once when the big earthquake struck Alaska and killed thousands of people. The second time when there wasn't any summer and there wasn't any pasture for the caribou and most of them starved to death. When we both have the same kind of dream it never fails."

The wrinkles in the old frog's face were like streaks of ashes. "Disaster and doom," he moaned.

"The crows are right," said Judge Black,

looking off where the animals who were leaving were having an early-morning meeting. "Fools rush in where angels fear to tread. Where there is no wood the fire goes out."

It took the animals about a week to get ready. All the while I was thinking and then I decided. I'd looked after Catfish Bend so long I couldn't let them go by themselves with all the terrible things I knew were going to happen. I'd go with them to California.

"The people and the animals in California are both crazy," said J.C., the fox, who wasn't any more anxious to go than I was. "It's all that sunlight. You know how people put pottery in the sun to harden. It hardens your brain the same way."

Now that I'd decided to go I heard other things besides what the white crows prophesied. There were rumors that some of the animals on the way disappeared mysteriously and never were heard of again. A few came through the Bend going east instead of west. They'd gone only a little distance and found too many hardships; they were on their way back home.

A couple of days before we started a queer thing happened. A bloodhound appeared at the edge of Catfish Swamp, a big, oldish bloodhound with shiny black hide and dangling ears so long they almost touched the ground; his face was mean as a hungry alligator. We'd seen bloodhounds before belonging to a hunter or looking for somebody escaped from jail. But they always stayed just a few hours asking questions—was the prisoner happy at home with his father and mother and what kind of animals did he run around with. After that they left.

This one didn't go away at all. He didn't bay like the other bloodhounds either—that terrible sound that made your heart stop

beating; we thought at first he was deaf and dumb. And he couldn't run like other bloodhounds. He had such a terrible limp in his right front paw, if he hadn't such a mean face you'd have really felt sorry for him.

I couldn't find out who he was till I talked to the old turtle who'd been around the Bend as far back as anybody could remember.

"He's the bloodhound they call the Tiger," said the turtle. "He was the fiercest bloodhound in the whole Mississippi Valley, the boss of the bloodhounds that worked for the Louisiana State Troopers at Baton Rouge. When the other bloodhounds lost a trail they'd always call the Tiger and he'd get the scent right away."

"His grandfather caught Pretty Boy Floyd," said a lady otter who'd come up dripping wet out of the river. "And they say he's much better. My grandfather knew his grandfather well. They say once he starts on a trail he never gives up. No matter how long it takes."

"He's always been mean," said the turtle. "But they say since the car hit him and broke his paw he's been ten times worse. A snake doctor treated him after he was hit and did an awful job. The snake doctor was used to treating only snakes, the other snake doctors said, and shouldn't have tried to treat any other animal. Most snake doctors can treat any kind of case, but he was the only one around."

"The way the bloodhound's acting he's

following somebody at the Bend," I said. "I wonder who."

I found out the next day when I was packing for the trip, taking extra supplies of apples and pears I'd borrowed from the porch where the lady at the farmhouse had put 'em out to ripen.

"I know who the Tiger's trailing," said the turtle who came hurrying over. "I heard him talking to a bloodhound that belongs to one of the hunters from Sugar Cane. I couldn't hear everything they said. But the animal he's tracking is you."

You could have knocked me over with a daisy petal. "What have I done?" I managed to ask. "What's he after me for?"

The turtle's head popped into his shell like a jack-in-the-box as a big rattlesnake crawled near, then popped out again as the snake moved off. "I don't know why. But I heard him say he'll get the goods on you if it takes a hundred years."

I guess I'd have worried a lot if I hadn't been busy getting ready to travel. We started out early next morning, moving down the riverbank, and I gave a final look at Catfish Bend. My throat was so choky I couldn't speak. I could see Judge Black and the old frog were holding back their tears. We were leaving the Bend, that had been our home for so many years, never to see it again in our lives. Even J.C., the fox, looked downhearted. But the young animals and the old ones with them who'd been anxious to go were happy. And so was our silly rabbit.

"I've written a new poem about it," said the rabbit, chewing a celery stalk. His poems were so bad they gave you a headache.

California, here we come.
Some animals are smart
And some are dumb.

Catfish Bend is nice
For mice
But—

We shut him up before he could finish.

"When I listen to your poetry I'm sorry I signed a pact not to eat you," said the fox. "Another one like that and I'll carry a new rabbit's foot. And I know what rabbit it'll be."

The rabbit gulped so hard the celery stalk dropped down his throat like he'd been a sword swallower in a circus. It took us almost half an hour of pulling and pounding to get it out again. I asked the fox to please take it easy.

The Bend faded from our sight. All morning we walked on slowly; with the turtle and the old animals we couldn't go fast. On the way we met other animals, all bound for Paradise Valley.

We sat down for lunch under a big

cypress tree.

"We've had a good morning," said J.C. "It looks like maybe things'll be all right after all. With good old J.C. along nobody has to worry."

Judge Black was more cheerful now. "Hope makes a good breakfast" he said.

Neither of them knew that before many days had gone by they'd find out they were terribly wrong.

2

We were still sitting under the tree when we saw some creatures coming toward us that didn't move like the others, some crickets and spiders, a few katydids and beetles, and behind them some grasshoppers and lizards. They came closer and then I saw why their walking was different; they were all blind.

"I guess you've heard of us," said a big grayish spider who was their leader. "We're the famous blind creatures from Mammoth Cave in Kentucky. Our ancestors were living in darkness so long they lost the use of their eyes. But we're tired of staying in a cave. We want to get to Paradise Valley."

"It isn't easy traveling when you're blind," said a katydid. Her voice was terribly sad. "Sometimes we come to a crossroads and walk a couple of miles before we find out we've taken the wrong turning. Unless somebody goes along with us and shows us the way I don't think we can travel much farther."

I hate to see anybody suffer so we said we'd put a Catfish Bend animal to walk with each one. That way it was like they had a seeing-eye dog: they couldn't go wrong.

We met more odd creatures that day. We stopped for a cooling drink at a brook rushing over some rocks. A brown and white pigeon was sitting there, splashing water on his feathers. His eyes were misty and red; you could see right off he'd been crying.

I asked him what was the matter.

"I'm a homing pigeon," he said. "But something's happened to my brain and I can't remember my home. I fly to a place thinking that's where I belong. And always I find I've gone wrong and get into terrible trouble. I just flew out to Little Rock, thinking maybe that was where I come from. But I landed among some pigeons that carried messages for some big moonshiners. They thought I was working for the U.S. revenue agents, and beat me until I could hardly stand. Maybe if you let me go along with you my brain will come back and I'll remember."

We couldn't see any reason why not so we told him yes.

It was almost dark when we saw a rattle-snake crawling toward the spot where we were making camp for the night. Judge Black, who was always so nice, hated rattlers worse than anything; he swelled up with his mouth wide open and his black tongue flashing and hissing like he was going to breathe fire. We all got ready for a battle.

But we could have saved our breath. When the rattlesnake came closer he was as pitiful as the homing pigeon and the creatures from Mammoth Cave. He was thin as a rail and there were ragged patches where scales were missing all over his body. "I'm a rattler from a snake-handling church back in the Tennessee Mountains," he told us when we'd calmed down and Judge Black was himself again. "I was a bad snake once and loved biting animals and people. But then a mountain preacher caught me and took me to the church and I got religion. That's why you see me in the terrible shape I'm in. I try to tell the other rattlers I meet they ought to change their ways. But most of the time they fight me."

Judge Black nodded that he agreed. "Other snakes treated me the same way when I became a vegetarian."

"I hope you'll let me go with you to Paradise Valley," the rattler went on.

"There's going to be a lot of wickedness and meanness there with so many animals. I want to preach to them and set them on the right path."

J.C., the fox, spoke to me quietly. "Don't let him come," he said. "He'll try to preach to us day and night. He'll be a terrible bore."

"He's suffered enough," said Judge Black. "He's a good snake. Let him join us. He who is stung by a scorpion has no fear of a house-fly."

Like always we didn't know quite what the Judge meant. So we let the rattler stay.

We ate our supper and I climbed up a tree for the night to be cool. I was just about to fall asleep when I heard a faint noise below me and I looked down through the branches. It was the bloodhound, the Tiger. He sat down in the grass, resting his crippled paw up in the air a little. I guess that way it didn't hurt so bad. He sat there all night, I guess. But when I woke up in the morning he was gone.

For a week we went down the river, sometimes walking along the bank, sometimes riding a log that'd drifted up on the shore. And every night after we'd pitched camp and eaten our supper the bloodhound would appear and take up a post near me. And just before sunup he'd limp away.

The land began to change now as we entered the Cajun Country. There were little rivers everywhere and big swamps and plenty of alligators. One night we stopped by a big lake; all around us you could see their eyes shining red, like hot coals fallen out of a fire. I counted a hundred alligators that way and there were plenty I missed. We put the watchman goose on guard as sentry. All geese have watchmen to warn them of foxes and any other enemies. This goose had been thrown out of his flock because he'd fallen asleep on his post. But since he'd come to the Bend he never had any trouble. He always carried coffee grounds he'd pick up outside a farm-house, or when he couldn't get these he'd fix up a couple of big pins he'd found and put them in a tree or wherever he was sitting so if he started to fall asleep and leaned back they'd stick him and he'd wake up.

A couple of times in the night he called out "Alligators!" and we'd see a couple of ugly shadows crawling toward us and we'd run for our lives. In the morning we called the roll; five of the Catfish animals and a dozen others who'd joined us on the way were missing.

We searched for them three days and nights and then gave up the search as hope-less. It made us all very gloomy for a while and some of the old animals talked about going back.

"I've lost my best tenor," moaned the old frog. "I trained him for a year two hours every day. The Club 'll never be the same

again."

We went deeper and deeper into the swamps. Big live oaks were all around us and cypresses with gnarled knees like hundred-year-old elephants. It was very scary. We went to sleep one night worrying about more alligators. But when we woke up in the morning we weren't thinking about alligators any more. Our heads were all burning as if somebody had lit gasoline and poured it inside; our stomachs were swollen like the big balloons they have at country fairs. We were so sick we thought we would die. I managed to send word by a muskrat

to the snake doctor I'd seen flying around the day before, and the muskrat brought back word he couldn't come.

"He told me they're terribly short of snake doctors here," said the muskrat. "He hasn't had a vacation in three years and he's worn out looking after all the animals on their way to California."

Judge Black was sicker than almost any of us; being so long and thin the way a snake is, when he's sick he isn't sick in any one place like the heart or the liver; he's sick all over. The Judge had been lying down, but he managed to get up and crawl toward the swamp. "I'll go and talk to him myself," he said. "A wise doctor does not live near a cemetery."

He went off and came back in a few minutes with the snake doctor flying over him. Even when Judge Black was sick everybody generally did what he said.

The snake doctor examined us all very carefully and made us put out our tongues.

He was young and talked very fast, not like most of the old snake doctors I knew. "Breathe deep and say a-a-a-h," he told us. His green wings flashed in the sunlight. I could see he was thinking hard.

"It's any one of ten things," he said. "It might be caused by your inhaling the breath of a big Congo snake sleeping near you. Or sleeping on green Spanish moss. You might have been bitten by a blister bug or stepped on a tarantula. You might have eaten green watermelon or swallowed fire ants. You might have been hit by a falling tree or stepped on a rusty nail. Or maybe clawed by a swamp wildcat or a possum with hydrophobia. I don't know which."

His wings flashed again like little streaks of lightning. "With old-fashioned doctoring I'd have to guess which sickness it was and half the time I'd be wrong. New-fashioned I'll give you a different medicine for each one of the ten and you take all ten

medicines together. That way I'll be sure to be right."

The ten medicines almost killed us, but in a few days we could travel again.

We left the swamps and went down into the marshes where the Mississippi flows into the Gulf of Mexico. They were scarier than the swamps with reeds fifteen feet high. If you turned your head the wrong way for a minute you'd be lost forever. We heard that the people there had lived in the marshes so long they had webbed feet like ducks so they couldn't sink in the spongy earth. They said the animals were the same way. But we never saw any.

The mosquitoes were terrible, so thick the people there called them smokestacks. The old turtle told us to swallow turpentine we could scratch from a turpentine tree; the turpentine would ooze through our skin and keep the mosquitoes away. We tried it a dozen times but all it did was give us the stomachache.

We hadn't seen the bloodhound for several days. Then a week passed and still there was no sign of him.

"It looks like he's gone," I said to Judge Black. "Now I can get some sleep at night. He made me terribly nervous."

The weather had changed, like the country. Big white clouds were always in the sky, as if somebody'd torn open some bales of cotton. Pelicans and gulls were always flying over our heads and there was always a smell of salt in the air. We could tell we were near the sea.

We were sloshing along a narrow trail through the marsh when we saw a big rattlesnake coiled beside a log, a whopper of a fellow almost twice as big as the one with us from Tennessee. His mouth was wide open, showing his wicked-looking fangs; he was hissing and rattling so hard you could have heard him half a mile away. But when we got near him we could see he wasn't terrible at all. Like the rattler from Tennessee he was really pathetic.

"My looking fierce is all an act," he told us, rattling all the time he talked, so loud we could hardly hear what he said. "If I didn't put on a show like this the other rattlers would find out my real condition and sting me to death. A rattler can't strike unless he's coiled from the right. I've been left-handed from birth. My mother did everything she could to change me but nothing did any good. I'll have to go this way the rest of my life. . . . Excuse me. I have to be impolite but I see another rattler coming. I'll have to rattle louder and show my fangs again. Or he might come by and investigate."

Like the Tennessee rattler he asked if he could join us. And being so sad the way he was we couldn't say no.

It turned out to be a good thing we let him come, because later that day we saw rattlers everywhere climbing what trees there were and crawling high up in the branches. Judge Black and the preacher rattler didn't know what that meant. But the left-handed rattler was from the marshes and told us right away.

"This is hurricane country," he said. He looked up at the sky where the white clouds were gray now, as if the cotton was dirty. "The snakes know a hurricane is coming and want to get away from the big water. The higher they climb the worse the hurricane'll be. I saw some of them in the tops of the trees. It's going to be a bad one."

"We had a terrible hurricane last year," said a muskrat who'd been watching from his little hut they call a college and came out when he saw the rattler was harmless. "Lasted three days and wrecked every boat along the coast, and killed I don't know how many thousand animals. You'd better do something fast."

"Only place you can get to in time is the shrimp platform near here," said the left-handed rattler. "I've been there twice my-self. It's run by the Chinese to dry their shrimp. The platforms cave in sometimes with the hurricanes but it's your only chance. If you hurry you can get there before dark."

We saw it just as the sun began to set, a wooden platform as big as a pasture, sitting on poles at the edge of the marsh. We climbed up and went off in a corner behind some old empty buildings where we figured people didn't come and so wouldn't see us. The sky was ugly now, with the clouds black as ink, and the wind was beginning to blow hard.

When we went to sleep the wind was howling like a hundred hungry coyotes. I woke up after a couple of hours with that funny feeling you have when you know something is wrong. I sat up on the old rope chest where I'd been lying and saw a black shadow stretched out on the planks near me.

I shook all over. It was the bloodhound.

He saw I was awake but didn't say any-thing. Just sat staring at me out of his hard green eyes.

I tried to get back to sleep but I couldn't. I stayed awake all the rest of the night.

As the day passed the waves got bigger and bigger. By night they were like black mountains. Every once in a while we'd hear a loud crash in the darkness as some part of the platform broke away. It was raining so hard now, with drops that seemed big as marbles, it almost knocked you down. I saw J.C. suddenly stand on his head and pretend to shiver. He winked an upside-down eye and shook the water from his dripping fur.

"I'm going to prophesy," he said, imitating the voices of the crows. "I prophesy it's going to rain."

The crows looked hurt.

You never knew what J.C. would do next.

Judge Black turned to the fox and shook his head. "There is a time to laugh and a time to cry," he said. "Fine fur may cover spoiled meat."

All of a sudden a wave came along so big it blotted out the sky. A minute later there was a new, terrible crash as the part of the platform where I was standing broke off and I found myself floundering in the water. Lucky for me I'm a good swimmer and was

getting close to what was left of the platform when I saw the bloodhound. By the way he was splashing around I could tell he couldn't swim a stroke. I couldn't see any animal die like that, no matter if he was my enemy, so I started swimming toward him.

"Keep your head up!" I shouted. "I'm coming to get you!"

When I reached him he was going down for the last time. Somehow I managed to get him onto my back and brought him to the platform. And I stretched him out and began pumping the water out of him. He opened his eyes after a while and lay there breathing deep, looking at me queerly. I thought anyway he'd thank me for saving his life. But he never said a word.

I saw now that a whole big section of the platform had crashed, throwing all the animals there into the water. I could hear them calling pitifully for help. I kept jumping in, trying to save as many as I could. All night we stayed there while more and more of the platform collapsed. Morning came and the waves began to grow smaller. I looked around and saw that Judge Black, J.C., the fox, the old frog and the rabbit and all our close friends were still there. But plenty of the others, maybe a third of those who'd come with us, were gone. The rattler from Tennessee that had gotten religion preached a funeral sermon. He preached too long the way J.C. said he would, and he got all excited and out of breath the way mountain preachers do, but I guess you can't expect too much in the middle of a hurricane.

We all cried a lot, and the Frog Glee Club sang *Massa's In De Cold, Cold Ground*, which is as sad as a song can be.

The water began to go down fast now. Suddenly we heard some cries for help coming out of a little building at the edge of the platform. We hurried over and saw what had happened. A few sea animals had been washed into the building and trapped there by some logs as if they'd been put in a pen. As long as the water was high they were all right. But when it went down, like any fish they wouldn't be able to breathe.

One of them was a big swordfish and he looked terribly fierce; his face was covered with deep scars. "Don't worry about the scars," he said when I told him I'd get the beaver to cut the logs and let him go back to the sea. "They're just dueling scars. We swordfish like to duel the way the German students did at Heidelberg. We're very proud of our scars."

There was a big grouper, too, must have weighed a hundred pounds, and an octopus, maybe four or five feet across.

"Free the grouper first. He may be hurt," the octopus said, and his voice was so soft and gentle at first I thought it must be some other animal. He talked to me while the beaver was cutting the grouper loose. I found out that he was like Judge Black. He was trying to live down the octopus's bad reputation.

"They call me the Angelic Octopus," he said. "I try to help the other sea creatures whenever I can. My father was a monster and killed plenty of fish and any animal that fell into the sea. I'm trying to make up for some of my father's sins. . . . Tell the beaver to free the needlefish and the parrot fish

next. They're hungry and I can wait."

I was getting everybody ready to start off again when the young raccoon I'd trained myself came up to me with the turtle. "We're leaving you," said the young raccoon. "You may have been smart once but now you're old and foolish. You've made a terrible mess of things and lost I don't know how many animals. We don't want you as a leader any more. We're going off by ourselves."

"He's right," said the turtle. "It's a young animal's world. Things have changed since you and I were young. The young turtles of forty and fifty are taking over. We old turtles and the other old animals are going with the raccoon."

I stood there, unable to speak. It was bad enough having the young raccoon turn like this against me. But that the old animals I'd done so much for would act the same way I could hardly believe. For the first time in my life I was losing confidence in myself. Maybe what they said was true.

Judge Black shook his head in sorrow. "O fiercer than the sting of the scorpion is the sting of ingratitude," he said.

The young animals and the old ones that had joined 'em formed a line and got ready to move off. I saw the young frogs in the Indian Bayou Glee Club stand hesitating for a minute; then they marched over to tell the old frog good-by.

He choked out a word I couldn't under-
stand. The tears rolling down his wrinkled
cheeks made his shiny face look like a
cracked mirror.

He watched the frogs march off with the
others, all the young animals and maybe half
the old ones.

"It's the end of the world," he moaned.
"I wish I was dead."

The two white crows had been watching
too. Then I saw them standing on their
heads and I knew they were going to
prophesy.

The husband began to talk first, and his
voice was very queer.

"I see some animals climbing a high
mountain," he said. "They are climbing
very slowly. And then I see the reason. All
the animals are blind."

The lady crow spoke now and her voice
was even stranger. "The animals climb and
climb, but they do not reach the top for

the mountain grows higher and higher. Then suddenly the mountain changes; the animals being blind do not see the change and keep on climbing." She began shaking so hard I thought her bones might break, the way I've seen people do that had chills and fever. "If the animals could have seen they would have rushed away in panic. For the mountain had become a terrible—"

The husband made a quick sign for her to be quiet. And I knew the reason. It was the same way with the old owl who'd been at the Bend. And I'd heard it was the same with the Gypsies, too. They always stay silent when the future is too terrible to tell.

3

I thought of turning back, even though we'd come a long way. But then I saw how anxious the old animals who'd stayed with me were to get to California and I knew it was my duty to go on.

We left the marshes not long after and came to a white sandy beach along the Gulf of Mexico. And then we saw a sign that said we were in Texas. There were a lot of snakes that had been washed up on shore from little islands just off the beach, ordinary chicken snakes and gopher snakes, but plenty of water moccasins and rattlers.

The left-handed rattler that was with us got very nervous. "You watch your step going along here," he said. "These Texas rattlers aren't like other Texans. Most Texas animals like to tell about Texas and show you how fine a place it is. But these rattlers are so proud and stuck on themselves they hate anybody doesn't come from Texas and don't like to have 'em around. And please let me go between you so they can't see me. If they saw a left-handed rattler like me I wouldn't last a second."

We did what he said and saw that he was right. Plenty of the rattlers were seven feet long and as thick as the trunk of a young tree. If you came anywhere near them they hissed like a bull alligator.

The minute we were in Texas there was a smell of oil everywhere; at night the sky was red from the flames that came from the places where they were making gasoline. Now we had a different worry. With all the oil wells around we couldn't find anything to eat.

By the time we got near Houston we were really starving. We were in the woods outside a little town that was one of the suburbs when an old bulldog with a nice friendly face came sniffing down a trail. He was so fat his stomach showed under him in heavy layers like rubber; his lower lip hung down the way bulldogs' lips always do and swung back and forth like a pendulum.

The minute we saw him he started talking about Texas. I asked him if he knew where we could get something to eat.

"That's easy," he said. "Everything here is the biggest and best anywhere. You're OK now you're in Texas. We Texans are famous for our hospitality. My master's a wonderful fellow. I saved his three-year-old boy from being killed in a fire and he gave me a charge account in the general store at the crossroads here. When I walk in the store I point my nose to what I want and they give it to me. I'll go there and get you some things and charge 'em to my account."

He left and came back in a few minutes

loaded down with all kinds of things to eat—
apples and bananas and packages of meat and
I don't know what all. He made three trips
and we really did some fine eating. And then
he made a fourth trip and came back out of
breath and looking awful. "My master happened to come to the store my last trip," he
said. "The clerk showed him the books and
all the things I'd charged and he went nearly
crazy. I'll have to collect the things you
haven't eaten and take them back."

He picked up the packages that were left.
"He's not a real Texan," the bulldog said
angrily. "He comes from the East somewhere, New York or Philadelphia. I heard
him say once his job there was putting people out of their houses when they couldn't
pay the rent."

We watched the bulldog hurry off with
the packages that would have kept us going
for a long time. But anyway we'd had a
good meal.

We went hungry for days, living on grass and a few berries we found. Some of the animals even ate the cactus that we'd see growing along the road. The spines would pierce their lips as if they'd bitten a porcupine. It wasn't so bad for the rabbit and the frog, but Judge Black and J.C. and I were getting thin as skeletons. Judge Black when we signed the pact not to fight told us to watch his eyes; if he was hungry and his lower nature was getting the better of him so that he'd forget he was a vegetarian, his eyes would get fuzzy around the edges. But whenever I looked they were clear as a beautiful diamond.

We got hungrier and hungrier. At night we'd dream about things to eat.

The rabbit sat up suddenly one night and gave a loud cry that waked us all. "I've just had a wonderful dream," he said. "I dreamt I was sleeping in a bed made of beautiful turnips and my blanket was spinach."

J.C., the fox, was very cross because he'd been wakened from a good sleep. "I've had a wonderful dream too," he said. "I dreamed I had a bowl of rabbit soup, and after that a dish of rabbit salad, and after that I finished off with a big plate of rabbit stew."

The rabbit fainted.

But the worst thing wasn't being hungry. What worried me most, though I didn't say anything, was the awful feeling always that something terrible was going to happen.

One good thing did happen that cheered us a little. We were walking through a little woods when we heard the sound of singing coming through the trees. The old frog stiffened as he stopped to listen. A minute later the singers came marching toward us; they were the young frogs of the Indian Bayou Glee Club of Catfish Bend.

The old frog's stomach began to swell the way it did when he was excited.

The young frog that had been the first

to say he wouldn't sing *Adeline* came up to the old frog and stood a minute looking miserable. "The young raccoon and the others threw us out," he said. "Some frogs from the Great Dismal Swamp out East that had a club came by and sang the new kind of music. All the animals began stamping up and down like they were crazy. We tried to sing it too, but we were no good. The young raccoon stopped us in the middle and said they didn't want us around any more. He said we were too old-fashioned."

The frogs didn't ask if they could come back. They just fell in behind the others. The old frog was so happy his stomach swelled so we had to stop and put cold water on him; we were afraid he'd burst.

We were getting farther west now. Cactus was growing all around us; people called it the Brush Country. Cattle ranches were everywhere, with big Brahma bulls that had sad eyes like they were going to cry any minute. It was hard crossing the ranches, trying to keep from being cut by the barbed-wire fences or getting caught on a cactus.

We were getting fewer and fewer. Almost every day one or two of the older animals couldn't stand the hardships of the trip any longer. They would stop along the road or wherever we were traveling, tell us good-by, and turn back.

The bloodhound was with us every night now; every sunset we'd see him come limping along on his crippled paw. He didn't bother to stay hidden from me any more. He'd fix a bed of grass or straw a hundred feet from where I'd be sleeping; that way he could watch me all night. The way he did before, he never said a word to any of us. Only when I'd come on him all of a sudden, he'd snarl and show his teeth the way a dogcatcher does when he throws his net and misses the dog he's chasing.

We camped for the night after a burning hot day on a big ranch that had hundreds of cattle. We ate our supper and tried to sleep but we couldn't; it was still so hot you felt you'd scorch your paws if you let them touch the ground. The cattle couldn't sleep either. All night the cows kept mooing; the bulls kept pawing the ground with their right foot, the way they do when there's going to be a big change in the weather. We could see the cowboys ringing the herd near us, trying to keep the cattle quiet.

"They're nervous because a Blue North-er's coming," said an armadillo lived on the ranch, who when he saw everybody was awake had come around for a chat. "I saw some black ants forming themselves into a ball today. I know my ants. I've eaten enough of 'em and that's the surest way to know somebody. When the ants make a ball of themselves it's the surest sign of a Blue Norther."

"What's a Blue Norther?" asked the silly rabbit. "I hope it has something to do with carrots."

The armadillo shook his head. "It's a wind comes down from Canada," he said. "There was a Blue Norther here a few years ago killed almost every animal on the prairie."

The cattle got more and more restless. One of the cowboys began to sing in a low voice, the way they do sometimes when the herd's so nervous.

"They're going to stampede," said J.C.,

the fox. "I'll sing to 'em myself. The cows on the farm in back of Memphis where I used to visit a friend always asked me to sing. They said my voice was very soothing."

"Do not fasten a big ship with a small anchor," said Judge Black. "We'll get the Glee Club to sing. They'll be better than you or the cowboys."

"It'll stop 'em from stampeding every time," said the old frog, who never missed a chance for the Club to perform. "I'll get them to sing *My Bonnie Lies Over The Ocean*. Cows like sad love songs. *Bonnie's* one of their favorites."

There was a little lake where the cattle came to drink. The Club moved to the bank and began to sing. For a few minutes the cattle grew quiet; it looked as if everything was going to be all right. Then suddenly a wildcat in the brush near us gave a terrible scream as it jumped to catch a rabbit or a ground squirrel. It was just as if somebody had dropped a bomb. The steers started running toward us, knocking down fences and young trees and everything in their path.

"Stampede!" I shouted, and we all started running to get away. Most of the animals got to safety in a hurry. But there was an old chipmunk and his half-paralyzed wife couldn't move fast, and I stayed behind to help. I got them out of the path of the charging cattle just in time. But the steers were right on top of me; I tried to reach a little clump of trees it wouldn't be easy for them to enter. But I was too late. A big steer knocked me down and raced squarely across my chest. I felt something snap inside me and then everything went dark.

When I came to Judge Black and the others were standing over me, looking very solemn, like people at a grave.

"We saw the steer run over you," said Judge Black. "We thought you were dead. The good die early. The bad die late."

I tried to stand up and fell down like a stone. "It's nothing," I said. "Maybe just a sprained paw. We've got to get on to Paradise Valley."

But they all knew I was lying.

Sunup came not long after. They found a sled of the kind farmers use to haul things and laid me on it. Then they started across the ranch again and all the animals took turns pulling. The day was even hotter than the day before; it was like when they opened the doors of the steel furnaces we'd seen in Houston. Then suddenly in the whisk of a raccoon's tail the sun went out; a bitter wind began to blow. Great chunks of hail, big as turkey eggs, began to fall. The trees, the mesquite, and the ground were white with thick layers of ice.

"It's the Blue Norther," said the armadillo, who was walking beside us for company. "You animals have to find shelter fast or it'll kill you all."

He thought a minute. "There's a big cave a couple of miles away where a lot of bats and snakes and turtles are living. We armadillos don't usually go there, but in a Blue Norther you take what shelter you can."

Judge Black and the others who had been pulling my sled started off in the direction the armadillo pointed. The wind was blowing almost as hard as in the hurricane; but now it was so cold my body seemed another layer of the ice coating the trees and the ground.

"You'll never make it if you have to drag me this way any longer," I told Judge Black. "Let me off the sled and I'll walk."

I persuaded them at last, and leaning on J.C. and Judge Black, struggled through the blizzard. Time after time I slipped on the ice and would have fallen if the others hadn't caught me. We came to the cave and went inside. The entrance was small, but the cave was as big as the railroad station I saw once in Memphis. Everywhere were all kinds of animals on the way to California, come to the cave to get out of the Norther—otters and skunks, and weasels and ferrets, rabbits and coyotes, and even a young panther. Big bats were hanging from the ceiling by the hundreds.

A few minutes after we got inside I fainted. When I came to again there were still more animals crowded around us, maybe almost a thousand; there was so much noise it was worse than when the cattle were stampeding.

We moved off to a corner where it was quieter. A big scorpion was there, maybe six inches long and three inches high. He jerked his tail upward the way scorpions do when they're ready to sting.

"Don't come so near me," he said. "I'm a scorpion from Durango in the mountains of Mexico. I'm more deadly than a cobra. And I'm very bad tempered. I heard a miner

in Durango say I'm like a mining truck
loaded with dynamite. I explode too easy."

I'd heard about Durango scorpions. So we
moved away in a hurry. Judge Black and
the others made a bed of straw, and I lay
down and tried to sleep. But my chest was
aching too badly; I wondered if I was going
to die.

We'd been in the cave a couple of hours
when a shadow appeared in the entrance.
The shadow turned and I saw a head with
ears drooping to the ground; it was the

Tiger, the bloodhound. He was covered with sleet from head to foot and spotted with clay where he'd slipped and fallen; he looked like a candy icicle I found once that a little boy had dropped in the mud.

"I'm with the police," he said to the big lizard standing guard at the entrance.

Those were the first words I'd ever heard him speak.

He limped inside and saw me lying in the corner and took his usual place close by.

The Norther lasted almost three days. The rattler from Tennessee tried to preach to the other animals, but they weren't interested. And the left-handed rattler never let the other rattlers see him coil. I told the homing pigeon to talk to everybody, thinking maybe by hearing the different ways they spoke he could remember where he came from. But it didn't do any good.

The creatures from Mammoth Cave who had come with us were feeling fine now,

even though they had left Kentucky because they were tired of caves. That way
animals are just like people. They get tired
of something and then when they don't have
it any more they couldn't be happier when
they get it back.

On the afternoon of the third day the sun
came out and made little rainbows on the
ice.

"Behind every cloud the sun is shining,"
said Judge Black.

My chest was aching worse than ever and
the Judge and the others wanted to carry
me on the sled again. But I insisted on walking. It was torture, but I knew if I didn't
they'd be so weighed down dragging along
a sick person we'd never get to Paradise
Valley. As we walked along I looked to see
how many animals were still with us. I
counted them carefully, one by one, and my
heart sank as I finished. More of our animals
had been lost on the frozen prairie in the

Blue Norther. Of all of us who'd started out from Catfish Bend now we were only thirty-two, not counting the frogs of the Glee Club. The thirty-two were mostly old animals that didn't have too many years left. For a minute I thought again of going back. But then I looked at their tired sad faces and I knew the vision of Paradise Valley was the only thing that kept them alive. I swore to myself I'd get them to California if ten minutes later I died.

Things were terrible, but once in a while something happened to make us feel better. We were walking along a narrow road when a little dogie—that's a motherless calf— came running out of the brush, sobbing the way a calf does, so hard you'd think his chest would burst. He asked like the others if he could come with us.

"They took me from my mother and sold me at auction in San Antonio," he told us. "But I ran away. I've nobody in the world that cares for me. Plenty of times I wish I'd have stayed with the man that bought me at the auction and he'd have sold me to the butcher."

He went along with us for several days. He tried to be cheerful but when he thought we couldn't see him he'd break down and sob the way he did before; he was always thinking of his mother. We came to a big ranch and I was asking the head bull if it was all right to cross, the way we always did, when the bull caught sight of the little dogie. The bull was a big tough fellow with a wide rip in one side I was sure he'd gotten in a fight. But when he saw the dogie his eyes lit up and he smiled.

"Your face looks familiar," he said. "And your voice sounds exactly like someone I knew. Are you off the Triple A Ranch near San Antonio?"

The dogie was terribly scared of the big bull but he managed to answer, "Yes sir."

The bull's smile became a wide grin. "I knew you were. You're the son of my sister they bought three years ago. You're my nephew." He studied the dogie's face. "You're the best bred stock in Texas. Don't worry any more. One of my wives will look after you."

The little dogie nudged against him. They went off together, like a happy father and son.

The country was getting wilder and wilder. We were near the border of Mexico now; a lot of the animals we met spoke Spanish. A bad thing happened to J.C. When he was asleep he was bitten by one of the vampire bats that flew over from caves in Mexico. Their bite isn't too bad, but the terrible thing is most of them have hydrophobia. I was scared to death J.C. would get it and go mad, the way dogs do in summer.

The fourth day after the vampire bite we

had just pitched camp for the night when J.C. came bursting from the mesquite with his mouth all foaming. "I'm mad!" he shouted. "Mad! Mad! Mad!" And he began dancing around like a horse that's eaten loco weed. "I'm a balloon!" he shouted. "A big red balloon blowing up! Stick a pin in me to keep me from bursting!" He took a big rusty pin he'd found somewhere and pretended to stick it in his stomach. And then he lay down and made a hissing noise, like a balloon makes when the air's going out.

I hurried to him as fast as I could with my bad chest to see if I could help. And then he jumped up laughing.

"I haven't got hydrophobia," he said. "I was only fooling. We've been so miserable and gloomy since we started I thought we'd have a little fun."

He wiped the foam from his lips with a paw; he'd made it with a bar of soap he'd found in a farmhouse. He was always a showoff, was J.C., and this was his idea of a joke. We all laughed a lot, but none of us thought it was really funny.

We got through Texas at last and went into New Mexico. Sometimes the country was nothing but desert; sometimes there were high mysterious mountains. We had a nice surprise when the big bald eagle who was the king of the birds at Catfish Bend flew out from Catfish to find out how we were getting on. We were glad to see him, even if he was sort of stuffy because he was the eagle on the silver dollar. He was walking beside me along a little trail when it was blocked by a herd of buffalo, one of those the government people started so the buffalo wouldn't die out. The eagle flew over them a few minutes and when he came back pointed out a big shaggy buffalo so bossy and proud you could see right away he was the head of the herd.

"He's the buffalo on the back of the buffalo nickel," the eagle said condescendingly. "Of course I'm the eagle on the silver dol- lar."

A little farther on we saw some Indians on their way to town to sell jewelry. A tall Indian was walking along, looking very im- portant, with a fat squaw behind him. "He's the Indian that was on the penny," said the eagle, more condescending than ever. "I met him when I was posing for the dollar in Washington."

I asked how things were at Catfish Bend. He said they were pretty terrible. All the regular animals were gone, he said; there was nothing now but a few cats from Sugar Cane who came there looking for mice.

The bloodhound was following us the way he always did. When we'd stop for the night I'd see him do setting-up exercises the way soldiers do in the Army, calling "One! Two! Three! Bend!" or "One! Two! Three! Twist!" and jerk out his head or his paws. I guess he was getting stiff from all the traveling. When we'd be near a town sometimes a couple of other bloodhounds would come out from the police station to see him, and they'd look over to where I happened to be, then would sit up with him all night, talking. One night they were so close I could hear them whispering, making some kind of a plan. Then they all started over to where I was lying as if they were going to arrest me. But something must have changed their minds; they wheeled around suddenly and went off in the direction of the town. Another night the blood-hound must have had a bad dream or something. Around second cockcrow he started baying the awful way a bloodhound does when he's following the trail of an escaped convict through the swamp. It made me feel as if my blood had stopped flowing and had turned into flakes of ice.

We were in the Hopi Indian country now in Arizona, with flat yellow hills they call mesas. The Indians here were very religious. They had little piles of stone everywhere with prayer feathers stuck in the top. When the wind made the feathers shake it was supposed to send the prayers to the Indian Heaven.

J.C., the fox, stopped to look at a circle of feathers with so many colors it was like a rainbow at sunset. "They're pretty," he said. "I think I'll steal one and put it in my hair."

"Please leave the feathers alone," I said.

"They're prayers and it'll be terrible bad luck."

But there was no stopping J.C. when he got started. He picked out a bright red feather and put it in his hair behind his ears, like the pictures I'd seen of mountain climbers in the Alps.

The bad luck came fast. It wasn't more than a couple of hours, I guess, when we saw a rocky peak not far ahead on the horizon.

"If you value your life keep away from that mountain," said an old lizard from the neighborhood who'd been walking with us a little way. "It's called Destruction Peak, and it's named right. It's full of terrible eagles that swoop down and fly off with you to feed their babies. Those young eagles are hungrier than alligators."

We were maybe a mile or so away when I saw the rabbit start sniffing and look off toward the mountain. "I smell carrots," he said, the way he always talked when he was going to do something crazy. "I'm dying for a carrot. I haven't had a carrot since we left Catfish Bend."

He sniffed again. "It is carrots. Big, sweet ones. On the side of the mountain. I'm going over to get them."

We tried to stop him but it was too late. Rabbits run too fast. He was maybe a few hundred feet from the mountain when I saw a big eagle swoop down, sink his claws into the rabbit's back, and carry him away.

We were all paralyzed with terror. "It's the end of the rabbit," moaned the old frog. "It's the end of the world."

Suddenly I saw our eagle from Catfish Bend who was staying with us for a while fly up from the ground near me. In a minute he was high in the air, pecking the eagle holding the rabbit with fierce blows of his beak. Feathers started dropping off the other eagle like a dusty rain; in a minute he'd had enough and turned to fly off. Our Catfish eagle snatched the rabbit from him and flew back to where we were standing.

He set the rabbit carefully on the ground and started to walk away. I hurried to thank him, but he shook his head proudly. "It's my duty," he said. "I'm the eagle on the silver dollar."

"Nobility shines like a lamp through a thousand dark curtains," said Judge Black.

The rabbit was all right, except for being scared. But I knew we hadn't begun to pay for that stolen prayer feather.

4

The next day it turned out was the day of the Hopi Snake Dance. Rattlesnakes were coming from every direction; they all acted as if they were hypnotized. They'd all been eating some kind of loco-weed the Hopis always gave them before the dance.

Both the rattlers with us were worried.

"When they have the dance the snakes always go crazy," said the left-handed rattler. "Afterward there's no telling what they'll do."

They had the dance on top of one of the mesas, with Indians in their fancy costumes handling the deadly rattlers like harmless caterpillars. There was a lot of beating of drums and the dancing got wilder. We could see our two rattlers were dying to join the others but they managed to hold back.

The dance was supposed to bring rain to the Hopi villages. And sure enough, right

after it was finished, the rain started to come down hard. It rained harder and harder and we moved off to a sheltered place under an overhanging cliff where the water wouldn't bother us. A lot of the rattlers were already there. They were all very nervous from the dance, but at first nothing happened. Then one of them, a big seven-foot diamondback, saw Judge Black. He crawled up to the Judge and began to get nasty.

"I don't like the way you talk," he said.

Judge Black turned away and didn't answer.

"You talk different than the snakes around here," said the diamondback. "I don't like snakes that are different."

Judge Black didn't pay any attention.

The diamondback crawled forward so the Judge couldn't avoid him. "I guess you're one of those smart-aleck snakes from the East I've heard about," he said. "We don't like your kind out here in the West."

The Judge still didn't answer a word.

The diamondback came so close to Judge Black his head was almost in the Judge's face. "I take that back. You're not from the East. You're just an ignorant Southern hillbilly."

Judge Black's long body quivered. But he still didn't say anything.

The diamondback pushed his head forward till their noses were almost touching. "I've always hated blacksnakes," he said. "They smell like goats."

I saw the Judge's eyes flash like lightning. Then he gave a terrific leap forward and caught the diamondback by the throat. In a minute the place went crazy. Diamondbacks came at the Judge from everywhere. He and our two rattlers fought hard, especially the preacher. He came from the Tennessee Mountains, and they'd had those what they call family feuds for years and years. But the Hopi rattlers were a hundred to three. Our snakes didn't have a chance. They dragged themselves away, the rattlers with plenty of their scales missing, and Judge Black so battered and patchy it looked like he was shedding his skin.

It was raining harder than ever now, but

we couldn't stay under the ledge any longer. The diamondbacks would have attacked and killed us all.

We went out into the downpour.

I turned to J.C., the fox. "Next time you start to steal a prayer feather, please quietly drown yourself," I said. I didn't often get sarcastic. But it was a terrible thing he'd done. And I was certain we weren't finished yet.

We crossed into Nevada and at last in some high mountains saw a sign, "Welcome To California." We all dropped to our knees; the old animals cried, they were so happy. They began dancing with each other in the middle of the road, though plenty of autos were passing. The old frog assembled the Glee Club; they sang *Star Spangled Banner*, and I never heard them sing so loud.

The old turtle was the happiest of all. "It looked as if we'd never make it," he said. "In no time we'll be in Paradise Valley.

Nothing can stop us now."

We spent that night beside an old miner's cabin high up in the pines. The old animals wanted to have a celebration. But I said they'd better wait.

"We have to cross Death Valley first," I said. "It's killed thousands of animals and people. We'll get there maybe tomorrow."

A gold miner was camped near us and the burro that worked for him came over to talk. He was so old his hair was white as the snow we could see on the distant mountains.

"I guess you heard of my great-grand-father," he said. "He's the burro that started the Gold Rush way back in forty-nine. He ran off from a mining camp and when they went to look for him they found gold. . . . I hope things are all right over at Paradise Valley. I've heard some funny rumors and yesterday I saw a lot of buzzards flying that way. I hope it doesn't mean that something's gone wrong. . . . You haven't got a chew of tobacco, have you? The miner Great-grandfather worked for didn't like to chew by himself so he trained Great-grandpa to chew with him. He said chewing kept his health going good. Great-grandpa taught Grandpa and Grandpa taught my father and Father taught me. But chewing tobacco today isn't what it used to be. Fact is, nothing's the way it used to be. I haven't had a good chew of tobacco since my father died."

I had fallen asleep not long after when I was wakened by a lot of noise in the cabin behind us. It sounded like a herd of horses running around on new iron shoes. I looked inside and saw it all came from a single, queer-looking rat racing over the cabin floor. While I watched he opened an old miner's chest, took out a candle that was inside, then put a stick of wood he found on the floor in its place.

I called out to him and asked why he was

stealing the candle.

He looked surprised that anybody was watching. "I'm not stealing," he said. "I'm a pack rat. We're just swappers. If we take anything we always put something in its place."

He hesitated, then added another stick to the first. "They call me Honest John," he said. "But the trouble is I lost my parents when I was young and never learned to count. I never remember how many things I took and how many I put back. . . . The last miner used this cabin was a bad one. I know where there's plenty of gold around here. Every night I'd leave him a nugget and he'd leave me a nickel for a trade. Then one night he got stingy the way people do, and instead of giving me a nickel he left me the cap off a bottle of soda pop. I can't count but I can sure tell the difference between a nickel and a bottle top. So next night I took all the nuggets back. . . . If you're crossing Death Valley you'd better go with me, otherwise you'll never make it. I have to see my brother at Stovepipe Wells. That's a good part of the way across."

I went to sleep and was wakened again at sunrise by the two white crows whispering. They were standing on their heads so I knew they'd been prophesying. They saw I was awake and jerked to their feet and didn't say another word. But I didn't need to hear any more. What I'd heard made my blood run cold.

We started across Death Valley a couple of hours later. It was like the pack rat said. If he hadn't been with us we'd have been lost before we'd gone half a mile. It was nothing but sand and rock, so hot the flies lost their wings and had to walk. Once in a while we'd see what they call a mirage; you thought you saw a beautiful lake with palm trees along the shore. When you came close it disappeared; there was nothing but drifting sand.

We reached Stovepipe Wells where there were people and where the pack rat's brother was living.

"I'm sorry I can't go any farther," the pack rat said. "They're having a pack-rat convention, and my brother who's the president wants me to make a speech on how not to lose when you swap. . . . Just keep heading west across the desert to the high mountains. I think you'll be OK."

We started out again and I guess things would have been all right if it hadn't been for the sandstorm. In a few seconds it was so black we couldn't see our paws before our faces; in a few minutes we were lost. The wind blew all day and night, then stopped in the morning. But we almost wished it hadn't. The sun was so hot when you touched your paw to the sand you could almost hear it sizzling.

We were getting terribly thirsty. But

there was no sign of water, only those strange mirages that now were everywhere. I remembered how the pack rat had said if we walked in the sun only a little while it'd dry up all the water in us and we'd die. We stopped in the shadow of some big rocks. But even there the heat of the sun was terrible. Near the rocks were the skeletons of maybe twenty people and two big dogs. I guess they'd been crossing the desert and gotten lost like us. We waited till the sun went down and started out again in the dark.

For a couple of days we wandered this way, moving only at night. We were almost dying of thirst; I think a lot of the time we were out of our heads. There wasn't anything alive around us now. Not an animal, a bird, or even an insect. Once we saw a kind of rat jumping on his hind feet like the kangaroos in Australia and we thought our troubles were over; if there was an ani-

mal around there must be some kind of
water. But when we talked to him we found
we were wrong.

"I'm a kangaroo rat," he said. "I hate
water. If a drop of water gets on my skin
it burns me like gasoline."

Then on the third day we came to the
foot of the beautiful Panamint Mountains.
And a wonderful cooling breeze blew down

on us, and I knew we were saved.

We rested a few days, then started up the mountains. I hadn't seen the bloodhound since we'd come to Death Valley and I thought this time we'd lost him for sure. But we'd only gone a little way when there he was behind us, limping along on his crippled paw. He'd come a different trail; 'course, being with the police he had all kinds of police dogs to show him the way.

Though it had been so dry in Death Valley it had been raining a lot in the mountains; every few hours we'd come on a big landslide. We'd see the earth and big rocks come tumbling down in front of us, rumbling like thunder. A couple of times we were almost caught, but we always jumped out of the way. We'd stopped for lunch and everybody was taking a nap except me, when I happened to look back at the narrow road cut out of the rock we'd been climbing for a couple of hours. The bloodhound was lying at the edge, sound asleep. And then I looked up and saw something terrible. The whole mountainside above him was cracking.

"Wake up!" I shouted. "Run for your life!"

He jumped up and saw me.

"Run for your life!" I shouted again. "The whole mountain's falling!"

He raced forward, just in time. A few seconds later the loosened earth crashed into the desert two thousand feet below. If I hadn't waked him when I did he'd have been buried alive.

He didn't say anything but I noticed his mean eyes got softer. Instead of glaring at me the way he always did he looked gloomy, just like the old frog.

It took us almost a week to cross the mountains. And every day the bloodhound got gloomier and gloomier.

We reached the final mountain at last.

By sunset we were almost at the top. The old animals were happy again. In the morning they'd finish the climb and see Paradise Valley. An old possum found a lot of food in a cupboard in an empty miner's cabin, some fine bread and cheese and some raisins and nuts and even some cookies and candy.

"Let's have a party," said the rabbit. And everybody agreed. J.C. did some of his fancy juggling and imitated a showboat calliope, and the Frog Glee Club sang till they were hoarse.

"Hope well and have well," said Judge Black. "It takes a long time to ripen good fruit."

We all lay down to get a little rest. But somehow I couldn't sleep. I counted sheep and possums and people, but none of it did any good. I couldn't close my eyes. I was worried, I didn't know why.

The road where we'd stopped wound around a cliff so high if you dropped a stone

you couldn't hear it hit. Suddenly I saw the bloodhound get up and walk to the rocky edge. He stood there a minute shivering; I could tell he was getting ready to jump.

I pulled him back just as he was going over. When his shivering stopped I asked him why he wanted to jump.

"Life isn't worth living any more," he said. "It was bad enough when you saved me in the hurricane. And now you've saved me from the slide I can't bear it any longer. My duty is to turn you over to the blood-hounds in Paradise Valley tomorrow. If I do I'm betraying the animal that saved my life twice. It tears me to pieces."

"What have I done?" I asked. "Why do you follow me this way as if I were some terrible murderer?"

He shook his head sadly. "It's that time in Opelousas, Louisiana. When you came with the trained-animal act in the circus and you bit the bloodhound that was track-ing your trainer after he stole the circus money. The bite you gave the hound was infected. He got blood poisoning and died."

His eyes glistened with tears. He brushed them aside with his crippled paw. "He was my closest friend. We'd been brought up in the same kennel and went to the same obedience school. I'd been retired, living in New Orleans, when I heard what happened. I swore vengeance and I began looking for you right away. And then a friend came through Catfish Bend and saw you and told me where you were living. There isn't a bloodhound in the country wouldn't attack you if he knew. Just the way policemen do when someone kills another policeman."

I looked at him and thought of all the nervous days and sleepless nights I'd worried so about him. And I breathed a sigh of relief so deep it hurt my chest.

"It wasn't me that bit your friend," I said. "That was a raccoon half brother of mine, the black sheep of our family. He looked exactly like me. I was never in Opelousas in my life."

I brushed the mud from my fur where I'd reached over the cliff to save him. "You'll never find my half brother now.

I heard a year ago the trainer took him along with a circus going to South America."

Well, the bloodhound was happy and sad. Happy he didn't have to arrest me, but sad he'd lost the animal who'd caused the death of his friend. That's the way it is with life, nothing's quite the way you expect it.

I was too excited after that to even try to go back to sleep. And in a little while the whole camp was awake and anxious to get to the top of the mountain.

"It'll be the Promised Land," said the old turtle. "I'll live here another hundred years."

We rounded the big rock that marked the top of the ridge and saw the whole valley spread out before us. And the sun seemed to suddenly turn black and our

hearts seemed to stop beating. Instead of the beautiful green plain we'd heard about with orange groves and plum and apricot orchards, as far as you could see was nothing but a terrible desert, sand and rocks and yellow clay. Everywhere were cracks maybe a foot wide where the dry earth had broken open. In places thick clouds of yellow dust were rising, with dust whirls like little tornadoes. Even at the top of the mountain we could feel the heat coming up in waves, the way it did in Death Valley. We'd all been fooled, just like the people we'd heard about who'd bought land in Florida and then found out it was under twenty feet of water.

5

At first everybody was so stunned they were like statues carved from the rocks around us. Then the old animals fell to their knees and began to cry like a baby otter I heard once when a hunter took it away from its dead mother that he'd shot. It broke your heart to hear them sobbing so. They had expected so much. Now they had nothing.

Maybe, I thought, there's a mistake. Maybe there's some fine place in the Valley we can't see when we're so high up on the mountain. But when we got to the bottom we found it was worse. The dust was blowing all the time, so thick you almost choked. The only living things were a few lizards, and they were panting for breath.

We found a pool of half salty water and stopped there for the night, trying to decide what to do. Suddenly we heard some familiar voices; a minute later we saw the young animals and the young raccoon who'd left us after the hurricane in Texas. They'd been camped up on the mountain for several days. When they saw us going down, they'd decided to follow. They were different than when we'd seen them last; all their smart-aleckness was gone. They'd had even more trouble than we had; they'd lost two-thirds of their animals on the way.

Next morning we began searching the Valley, still hoping we could find some hidden canyon or prairie that was the paradise we'd expected. Here and there we'd find a few clumps of stunted trees, trying hard to stay alive. But that was all.

We weren't the only ones who'd been tricked this way. The Valley was full of animals who'd come from all over the country; deer and foxes and wild pigs and beavers and even some caribou from Canada. And there were people, too, had been fooled just like us, and come in cars and trucks and trailers. And like our old animals, where there were old people you'd be sure to see somebody crying.

I waked in the middle of our second night with the same feeling I'd had before that something was very wrong. I called out to Judge Black and J.C. and the bloodhound who was sleeping near me. Since the bloodhound had learned the truth he and I had become fast friends.

"There's something queer going on," I said. "I don't like the way we were brought here, under false pretenses. I don't like the way when you ask, nobody knows how it started. I don't like the way I saw that big flock of buzzards flying over us today. I won't stop till I find out why."

"Look twice at a two-faced animal," said

Judge Black.

"Old J.C. will find out," said the fox. "You can rely on good old J.C."

We found out what was wrong quicker than we expected. When we did we wished we hadn't.

We decided to mount guard and I was first on watch. The only thing I saw were a few big tarantulas crawling over some stones. But after breakfast we heard that two wild pigs and the caribou camped near us had disappeared in the night. We hurried over to investigate and found some big paw marks right by where they'd been sleeping. I didn't have to look twice to know who'd made those paw marks. They were the paws of a big panther.

The next night there were the same paw prints and a young deer, another wild pig, and an old rabbit were missing. I wanted to get our animals out fast and go back to Catfish Bend. But the old ones wouldn't agree. "We're too tired," the old turtle said. "It'll take a month or two to get our strength back. To climb those mountains again would kill us."

The next night the blow struck home. Three of our possums were missing. And the watchman goose was gone. This time the paw prints were different, two wildcats working together. All day we searched for the watchman goose, but we lost his trail at the edge of a deep canyon. There'd been a strong wind blowing for hours, piling up sand everywhere, so even the bloodhound was helpless.

"We can't leave after this," I said. "Even if the old animals would be willing. The goose has been a faithful friend. We can't desert him now."

Another night passed with two more animals gone, this time the silly rabbit and the beaver. And all around where they'd been sleeping were the marks of a big pack

of coyotes. We searched for them just like we did the goose. But we had to give up the same way; the trail ended at the canyon entrance.

"There's something in back of it all," said the bloodhound. "It's what we policemen call a crime pattern."

We made our guard tighter but when morning came we'd been dealt a terrible blow. J.C. was missing with half a dozen young raccoons and a couple of half-grown otters. This time the paw prints were crowded together—the big panther, the two wildcats, and the pack of coyotes again.

We'd gone to the canyon and were heading back to our camp when a possum and a muskrat came rushing out of the bushes. They were fat, but it was an unhealthy fat, with their faces all swollen like they had a toothache and their eyes all puffy the way pigs are when farmers are feeding them to get fat bacon.

"Hide us! Quick!" the possum panted. "We've just escaped with our lives!"

"You've got to get away fast or they'll kill you all!" burst out the muskrat. "They've got a big stockade on the side of the mountain a mining company built for their mules. It's full now of hundreds of animals. They're fattening them the way people do turkeys before Christmas."

"It's the big meat eaters," the possum panted. "The panthers and the wildcats and the coyotes and the eagles. The good open country around here's getting smaller and smaller, so there are fewer and fewer animals for the big ones to live on. They were all almost starving when this big panther came and showed them what to do."

"He was born in a zoo in Hollywood where they trained animals for the movies," said the muskrat. "He went bad after a couple of years and they moved him to Yellowstone Park. And then he began attacking the people in the park and the wardens moved him here."

"He's the wickedest panther in the West," panted the possum. "And the smartest. He knows all the city people's tricks. He saw how many people were buying land and coming to places like Paradise

Valley. He figured he and his friends could start the same kind of stories among the animals and then they'd come here, just like the people. And he and the other panthers and the wildcats and the coyotes would have a party every day."

"He's got you in a trap," said the muskrat. "He's got every road blocked so you can't get out. You're done for."

I decided I'd see that stockade for myself. Judge Black said he'd go along; when it was dark we crept up to the canyon entrance and went up the side of the mountain. We saw the stockade and all the animals inside—the caribou and the wild pigs and the others. Most of them were terribly fat, with puffy eyes and faces like the muskrat and the possum. For maybe a month they'd done nothing but sleep and eat. We crept around the stockade till I saw our rabbit chasing a white moth in the moonlight. And then I saw J.C., juggling some bottles and things he'd found on a trash pile for a crowd of turtles and squirrels. Not far away I saw the watchman goose, so sad and mournful his head that he always held so high was almost hidden in the grass. Near him was the beaver, sharpening his teeth on a stone. I wished we could get a word to them, but of course I didn't dare.

We went on and then I saw something that made me shudder. Maybe twenty or thirty buzzards with bulging stomachs were

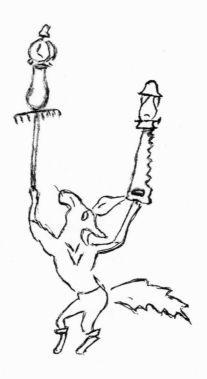

roosting in a tree; sitting that way in the branches they looked like ugly night flowers.

We kept on moving outside the stockade fence and then I saw the panther. And I needed only one look to know that what the muskrat said was true; he was the smartest and wickedest panther in the West. Like other panthers his tawny skin was smooth as silk; he moved as if he were made of velvet. But it was his eyes that were different. They were so slippery and so shifty they made you dizzy. I'd met slippery animals before, tricky ferrets and weasels and mink. But he was the slipperiest of all. He reminded me of a big rat I saw in a trap on the docks in New Orleans where he'd been stealing grain for a year; the other rats said he could steal the teeth out of your mouth and you wouldn't know they were gone till you started to chew.

Every once in a while the panther would

pinch a wild pig or a deer to see how it was fattening; he'd get a look in his eyes that made you shiver. Around his neck was one of those little radio sets game wardens put on an animal so they know where he is any minute. Every once in a while the panther'd rub against a tree, trying to get it off.

He was near the fence talking to a big wildcat I could tell was his assistant. I stopped to listen to what they were saying.

"We'll get the rest of those animals from Catfish Bend right off," said the panther. "Specially that raccoon and the blacksnake. If we don't we'll have an alligator by the tail, the way they say. I can tell they're real troublemakers." He rubbed the radio set against a tree again. "If I ever catch that warden put this thing on me I'll put him in the stockade with the other animals and have him for a Sunday dinner."

"We better make a big raid on those

Catfish Benders and the others pretty quick," said the wildcat. "All the animals down there in the valley are getting more and more restless. We've got to teach 'em a lesson."

"You teach a few of 'em a lesson and the others 'll follow like sheep," said the panther. "The way I was brought up I know animals and people both. Neither of 'em are very bright."

We made our way back to the Valley and all night tried to think of a plan. But it was as if we were in a thick fog; our brains were dead. I didn't eat breakfast or lunch. When you don't have food, the snake doctors had told me, your brain is quicker and clearer. But it didn't help. It looked as if the panther was right; we weren't very bright.

It was late in the afternoon when the muskrat we'd talked to the day before came running up with a younger muskrat beside him. "This is my young cousin from near Baton Rouge," he said. "He's just escaped from the stockade. The panther's getting all the big animals together; they're coming on a big raid at midnight tonight. My cousin heard the panther say when they get through, in the whole Valley there won't be a single animal left."

The sun set and it grew dark. Here and there you could see a fire blazing where some of the people who had come West had made camp and were eating their supper. And then I remembered the time some gangster rats came down from Chicago to Catfish Bend and said they were taking it over. And I knew now what we had to do. It was a risky plan. If it went wrong it could kill us all.

We picked out a half-dozen animals we could trust not to talk and began gathering dry leaves and dead mesquite and straw. And we put these at the canyon mouth till we had a pile twice as high as a deer. And then we sat in the shadows, waiting. We could hear the big animals moving around, gathering in the canyon. They were trying to be quiet but from the noise they made we could tell there were a couple of hundred.

Near the end of the canyon were a dozen fat men and women come out to the desert from the town close by, having a barbecue. Toward midnight we moved to the bushes beside the fire, so near we could almost taste the chicken they were eating. Then suddenly, near midnight, the canyon was deathly silent; the big animals were getting ready to charge. I whispered a signal. A second later I and a few others rushed at the campers, screaming at the top of our lungs. The campers were all city people and ran for their lives; they were sure they were being murdered. Their fire was blazing in the barbecue pit; it was the fire, not the people, we were after. A can full of kerosene was standing a few feet away; we poured the kerosene like a fuse to the straw at the mouth of the canyon. It shot up like an exploding volcano. In a few seconds the whole canyon was blazing. There was a single tree, a towering pine, a little way from the entrance. I climbed it fast; from the top I could see the panther and his friends racing toward the other end of the canyon just ahead of the flames. None of them were really burned. They were too fast for that. But I don't think I'm mean when I say I was happy to hear the panther roaring his head off as he ran and to smell the smell of scorching fur.

The fire didn't burn long. It was only brush and there was a forest ranger's fire tower nearby; the rangers came in a hurry the way I figured they would, and put it out. But I knew now we were safe. I knew the panther and his friends wouldn't dare to come back where people were camping with all the rangers around.

We hurried up to the stockade and let all the animals go. And we found J.C. and the rabbit and the goose and the beaver and took them back to our camp.

"That was a great plan I made to get rid of the panther," J.C. said to me. "I plan and you carry out. That's a fine combination. If you hadn't come when you did I'd have had all the animals out anyway. I had a plan that couldn't fail."

I didn't say a word. I only looked at Judge Black and smiled. We all knew J.C.

The rangers were going to fine the fat people for being careless about the fire. But they let 'em go when the fat people said they'd been attacked by a dozen panthers and twenty grizzly bears.

The panther tried to hide in the thick timber up the mountain; but with the radio on him when the rangers started searching they found him right away. They said they couldn't take any more chances. So they trapped him again and moved him and the others to a forest way up in Oregon, hundreds of miles from anywhere.

'Course the attackers had been us—a raccoon, a blacksnake, a frog, a muskrat, and a few other animals wouldn't hurt a flea.

But that's the way people are.

After the fire we had another party, a real celebration this time. J.C. did an imitation of the panther running away that was so funny we made him do it three times. We'd heard there were some frogs in the mountains that were fine singers had a club called the Sierra Glee Club, and we invited them to the party. They came and sang together with the Indian Bayou Glee Club, and it was the most beautiful music you ever heard.

We stayed in the Valley a couple of days, making up our minds what we'd do. And almost everybody said they'd go back to Catfish Bend. The young raccoon and a few of the others said they'd go to Los Angeles and San Francisco. They wanted to see the big towns, they told us, so we didn't try to argue. The rattler preacher from Tennessee said California was a wonderful place for preachers, so he'd stay there too. The blind cricket and the others who'd come from Mammoth Cave said since they were out West they'd visit Carlsbad Caverns in New Mexico and see how they got along there.

Some big trucks carrying freight for Florida were crossing the desert and stopped near our camp. We crawled inside and in a few days were back on the banks of the Mississippi. And then we saw Catfish Bend, with its wonderful live oaks hung with Spanish moss and the blue jays and the redbirds flying through the branches. And beyond the live oaks the beautiful green pastures for the cows, and the melons and

the peaches just ripe for an animal to borrow. And the old animals cried again, but
this time because they were so happy.

"This is what we've been looking for,"
said the old turtle. "This is the real Paradise
Valley."

Afterward things couldn't have been better. Catfish Bend was more wonderful than
it had been before. Each day some of the
animals we lost on the way to California
came back until there was hardly anybody
missing. You had to almost fight any animal

from Catfish Bend to get him to leave long
enough to go to town. And that's only two
miles away.

The bloodhound liked it so much he decided to stay. He turned out to be a wonderful animal; every night we sat in a circle around him, listening to him tell stories of the criminals he'd captured. And the homing pigeon stopped searching for the place he came from; now Catfish Bend was home. The left-handed rattler decided to stay too. So as not to cause any trouble he became a vegetarian, like Judge Black.

We were all having supper a while back when a cat we know walked over from the farmhouse at the edge of town, a big Tom with two black spots around his eyes made him look a little like a raccoon. He came out once a week or so with pies or cakes he'd brought from the farmhouse to swap for a nice catfish.

"I just heard today my people are going to Florida," he said. "I'm going with 'em. Does anybody here want to go along? There'll be plenty of room in the pickup."

For a minute nobody answered. Then
we looked at each other. And we laughed
so hard you couldn't have heard it thunder.

****

The raccoon finished his story. "That was a month ago," he said. "And like I told you we've all been very happy. And then this new fad that's all over the country came along, to make everything bigger. And now things may be different. Those two foxes and the beavers you saw chopping the trees came down from the North with a fancy plan to dam Indian Bayou and make the Bend ten times the size it is now. They say with the dam the Bend can have five hundred more animal families with a beautiful lake and fine new holes and swimming pools and all kinds of excitement going on every minute. The way I said the foxes are good talkers and some of the animals have been listening. Judge Black and J.C. and the rest of us are against it; we know the Bend would be ruined. But we do things the majority way at the Bend. So that's why we're having an election."

I came back late in the afternoon, and I could tell the election was over. Animals were standing around in little groups, talking and joking. And then I saw the two foxes and the beavers, walking slowly toward the road to town. They looked as gloomy as if they were on the way to their own funeral.

"How did it go?" I said when I met the raccoon, though I really knew without asking.

The raccoon was all smiles. He looked at the two piles of stones under a big live-oak tree that were the ballots for the voting. "It was wonderful," he said. "There were four hundred and sixty-one votes for us and one vote for the foxes. The one vote was an old skunk. He was mad because we'd forgotten to invite him to a party."

It made me remember what I too often forget. Plenty of times animals are smarter than people.